Runaway John

by Leonore Klein

illustrated by Sunny B. Warner

Alfred A. Knopf : New York

To JOE, JUDY, and BOB, with love

L. C. catalog card number: 63-14422

This is a Borzoi Book, Published by Alfred A. Knopf, Inc.

John stood in his yard one day.
It was a gray and grumbly day. John felt
gray and grumbly, too.
"I know," said John. "I'll run away
from home. That's what I'll do."

So John filled a bag with apples and cookies and bread-and-jelly sandwiches and put it neatly on the steps of the porch.

"If I run away from home," said John, "I'll have to sleep. I'll need something warm for a cover at night."

So John folded a blanket and puffed up a pillow
(for his head to rest on). He put the blanket and
pillow on the steps of the porch.

"If I run away from home," said John. "I'll have to hunt and fish. Everyone who runs away from home hunts and fishes."

So John put his gun and his fishing rod together
with the blanket and the puffed-up pillow and
the bag of apples and cookies and bread-and-
jelly sandwiches on the steps of the porch.

Then John said, "If I run away from home, I'll
need my dog. I'll need him for hunting and be-
cause he'll miss me."

So John woke up Towser, and fastened a leash to Towser's neck. Then he tied the leash to the railing near the steps of the porch.

"If I run away from home," said John, "I'll need things to play with once in a while."

So John filled a box with his bat and ball, his toy soldiers, and his checker set. He put the box on the steps of the porch, next to Towser, his dog, who was next to his blanket and pillow,

which were next to his gun and fishing rod, which were next to the bag filled with apples and cook-ies and bread-and-jelly sandwiches.

"If I run away from home," said John, "I'll need someone to play with. I can't play checkers by myself."

So John ran to William's house and asked William to run away from home with him, and William agreed to run away from home with John. He and John came back to John's porch.

"I'm almost ready to run away from home," said John.

Then, suddenly, John remembered something very important.

"If we run away from home," said John, "We'll need someone to tell us a story at night. Mother," called John, "will you run away from home with us?"

"I'll be glad to run away from home with you," said John's mother, and she joined John on the steps of the porch. "Shall I leave a note for Daddy about our running away from home?"

"Daddy!"

John had forgotten all about Daddy.

"If I run away from home," said John, "who will bring Daddy his dessert?"

John couldn't ask Daddy to run away from home with him. Daddy was at work.

"And if we run away from home," said John to
his mother, "Daddy will be all alone."
What could John do?
He thought and thought.

"You know what," said John to his dog, Towser, to his friend, William, and to his mother, "I'll run away from home some other time, when Daddy can run away with us, too. I think I'll just stay at home today."

"That seems like a good idea," said John's mother
and his friend, William.

And John's mother, and his friend, William, and his dog, Towser, decided to stay home with John. They decided to run away from home with John some other time.

Text set in Melior. Composed by Philmac Typographers. Printed by Reehl Litho., Inc. Bound by Economy Bookbinding Corp. Typography by Atha Tehon.